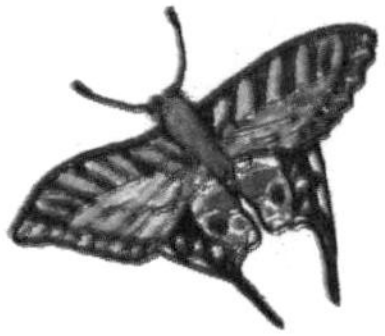

Have You Seen My Duckling?

Nancy Tafuri

MULBERRY BOOKS · New York

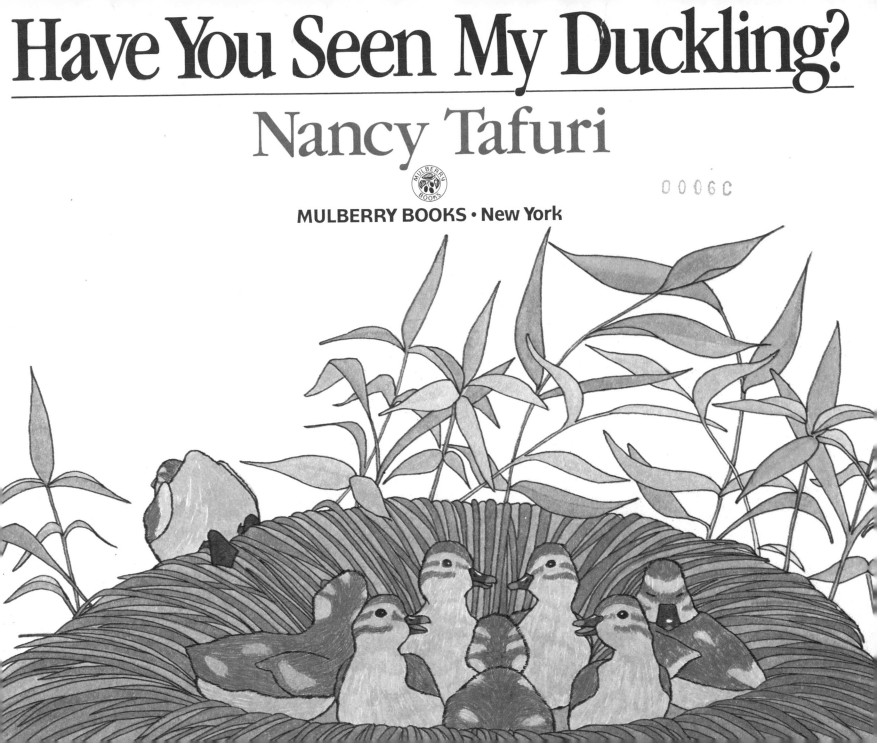

To the little duckling in all of us

Publisher. Greenwillow Books,
a division of William Morrow
& Co., Inc., 1350 Avenue of the
Americas, New York, N.Y. 10019.
Printed in U.S.A.
First Mulberry edition, 1991

Library of Congress Cataloging in Publication Data
Tafuri, Nancy: Have you seen my duckling?
Summary: A mother duck leads her brood around the
pond as she searches for one missing duckling.
[1. Lost children—Fiction. 2. Duck—Fiction. 3. Ponds—
Fiction] I. Title. PZ7.T117Hav 1984 [E] 83-17196 —

Early one morning...

Have you seen my duckling?

Have you
seen my
duckling?

Have
you seen
my duckling?

Have you seen my duckling?

Have you
seen my
duckling?